But Grandma Didn't Mind

By Nancy Rose Brekke

Design by Dawn Armato-Brehm

Rosebud Books from Raven Productions, Inc

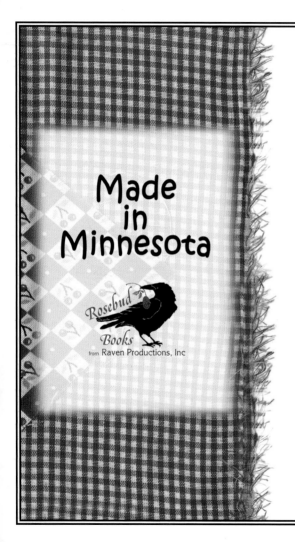

Made
in
Minnesota

Rosebud
Books
from Raven Productions, Inc

Printed in the USA
10 9 8 7 6 5 4 3 2 1

Library of Congress Cataloging-in-Publication Data

Brekke, Nancy Rose, 1958-
  But Grandma didn't mind / by Nancy Rose Brekke ; design by
Dawn Armato-Brehm.
     p. cm.
  "Rosebud books."
  Summary: A young boy has a wonderful visit with his patient and
loving grandmother.
   ISBN 0-9766264-0-3 (alk. paper)
  [1. Grandmothers--Fiction.] I. Title: But Grandma did't mind. II.
Title.
  PZ7.B7496But 2005
  [E]--dc22
                                          2005004841

The inspiration for my book
came from my Mom,
Betty Schram, who is
"Grandma Betty" to all fifteen
of her grandchildren.
Betty is the daughter of the
Grandma in my book,
"Grandma Jenny."

This book is dedicated
to my husband, Lee,
and sons, Robbie and Ethan.

Watch for these other
ROSEBUD BOOKS
by Nancy Rose Brekke

But That's OK with
Grandpa

Cause That's
the Way I Am

Cause She's
My Sister

Cause I'm
Mama's Favorite

Grandma called and
asked if I could spend
the night at her house.
Mom said, "YES!"
I was so excited!

I packed my bags to go
to Grandma's house.

As we drove
to Grandma's house,
I wondered what kind
of cookies Grandma
would be baking today.

As soon as I walked into her house,
I knew – it was chocolate chip.
MY FAVORITE! As I dipped my third
cookie in milk, I thought I probably
should not eat any more cookies,
or I would spoil my supper.
BUT GRANDMA DIDN'T MIND.
My fourth cookie was even better
than my first three.

Then Grandma let me paint a picture. I got excited and accidentally spilled the blue paint all over her flowered tablecloth. BUT GRANDMA DIDN'T MIND.

After we put the paints away,
it was time to get ready for dinner.
Grandma made my FAVORITE –
chicken dumpling soup.
We sat down to eat.
I was so hungry! I swallowed
a big steamy spoonful of soup.
Then I remembered that
I didn't wash my hands.
BUT GRANDMA
DIDN'T MIND.

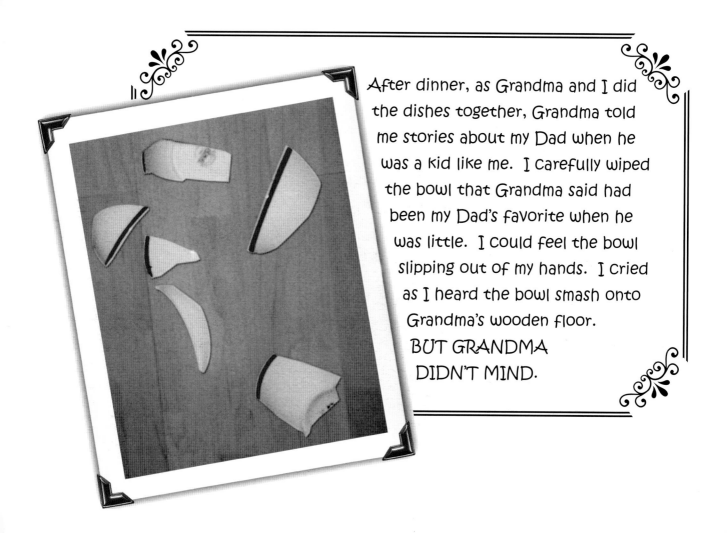

After dinner, as Grandma and I did the dishes together, Grandma told me stories about my Dad when he was a kid like me. I carefully wiped the bowl that Grandma said had been my Dad's favorite when he was little. I could feel the bowl slipping out of my hands. I cried as I heard the bowl smash onto Grandma's wooden floor.
BUT GRANDMA DIDN'T MIND.

Then Grandma took out her old pictures and we sat down on her worn comfy sofa.

I loved looking at
old pictures of my Dad.
I thought to myself,
"I kind of look like him
when he was my age."
He even had a
big brown dog too.

Grandma and I had so much fun looking at pictures that Grandma forgot to check the time. I think she forgot on purpose. When we heard her old clock chime twelve times, we crawled into bed. I hardly ever get to stay up till midnight. BUT GRANDMA DIDN'T MIND.

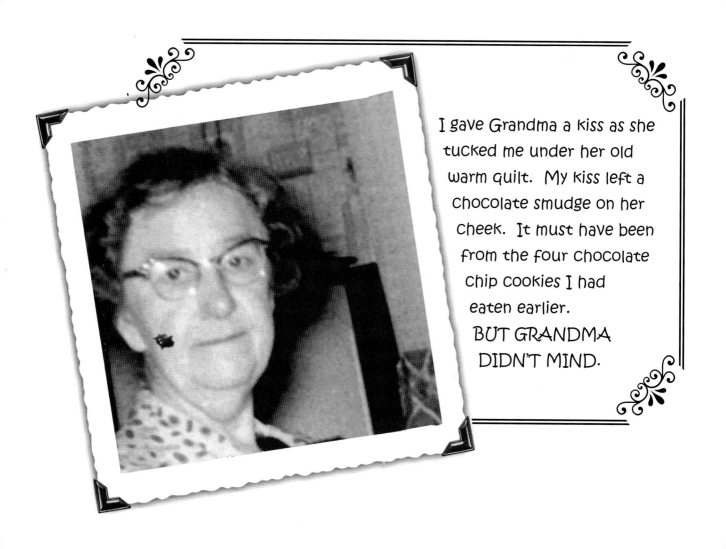

I gave Grandma a kiss as she tucked me under her old warm quilt. My kiss left a chocolate smudge on her cheek. It must have been from the four chocolate chip cookies I had eaten earlier.
BUT GRANDMA DIDN'T MIND.

I fell asleep and was dreaming about my Dad when he was a little boy sleeping in this bed. I think I even snored a little. BUT GRANDMA DIDN'T MIND.

I woke up to the smell of Grandma's buttermilk pancakes. I was so hungry I ate five. Then I ate one more with extra syrup, extra butter, and even chocolate sprinkles on the top. Then I noticed that I had spilled sticky syrup down the front of my shirt. BUT GRANDMA DIDN'T MIND.

So after breakfast, I put on a clean shirt and hurried outside to play. Then I remembered that I didn't put my sticky shirt in the clothes hamper. BUT GRANDMA DIDN'T MIND.

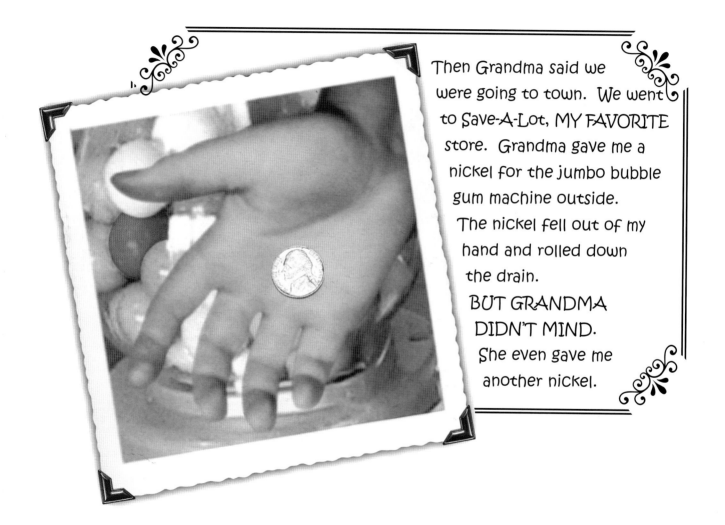

Then Grandma said we were going to town. We went to Save-A-Lot, MY FAVORITE store. Grandma gave me a nickel for the jumbo bubble gum machine outside. The nickel fell out of my hand and rolled down the drain.
BUT GRANDMA DIDN'T MIND.
She even gave me another nickel.

After shopping, we carried the groceries to the car. I told Grandma I was old enough to carry the bag myself. But the bag got too heavy. I didn't know the eggs would fall out and break. BUT GRANDMA DIDN'T MIND.

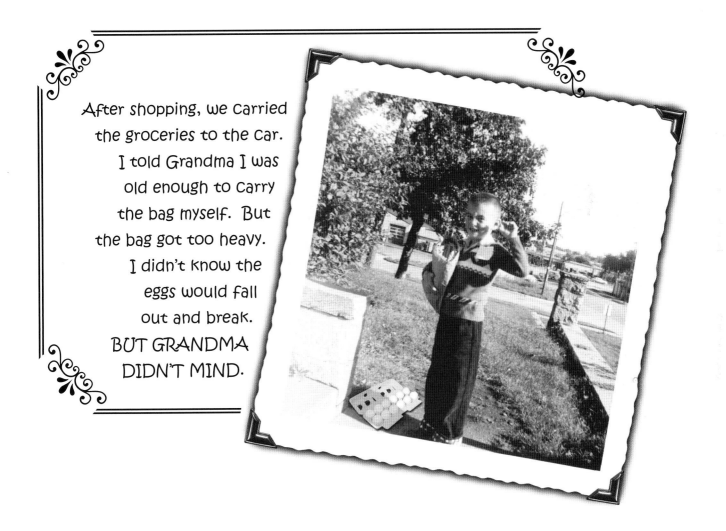

As we were driving back to Grandma's house, I started thinking about my family. I even missed my sisters a little.

When we pulled into Grandma's yard, I told Grandma I missed my family and wanted to go home. I didn't want to hurt Grandma's feelings, BUT GRANDMA DIDN'T MIND.

When we got to my house,
everyone ran out to meet us -
even my sister! I gave
everyone a BIG FAT HUG!
Then we all gave Grandma
a BIG FAT HUG too!
BUT GRANDMA
DIDN'T MIND.

Then Grandma said that it was getting late, so she'd better be going. We all gave her a big wave as she drove away.

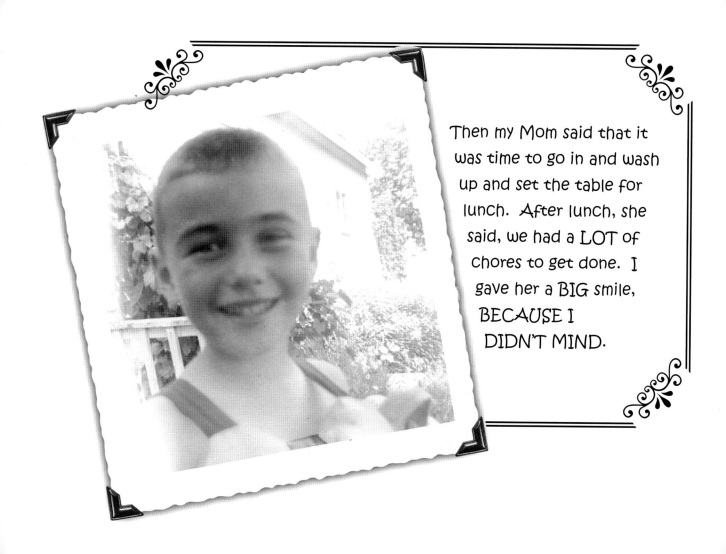

Then my Mom said that it was time to go in and wash up and set the table for lunch. After lunch, she said, we had a LOT of chores to get done. I gave her a BIG smile, BECAUSE I DIDN'T MIND.

MY Grandma didn't mind when I ...

My favorite things to do with MY Grandma are ...

_____

_____

_____

_____

_____

_____

_____

_____

_____

_____

Here is a picture
of MY Grandma
and ME!